# The DIDDLYS

## STEAM-POWERED SUPERHEROES!

# Tropical Trouble

RR
RAVETTE PUBLISHING

Created by Kevin McCluskey
Written by Caroline Petherbridge
Edited by Gordon Volke
Illustrated by Simon Hamblett & Tony Tinsley

visit the Diddlys website: www.thediddlys.co.uk

First published by Ravette Publishing 2004.



Ravette Publishing Limited,
Unit 3, Tristar Centre,
Star Road, Partridge Green,
West Sussex RH13 8RA

ISBN: 1 84161 202 2

TING-A-LING-A-LING!

"Is that the alarm?" groaned Diddly Dee, opening her eyes.

"No," replied Criss Cross, the signal. "It's my bell. Sorry if it woke you up. This strong wind is making it ring really loudly!"

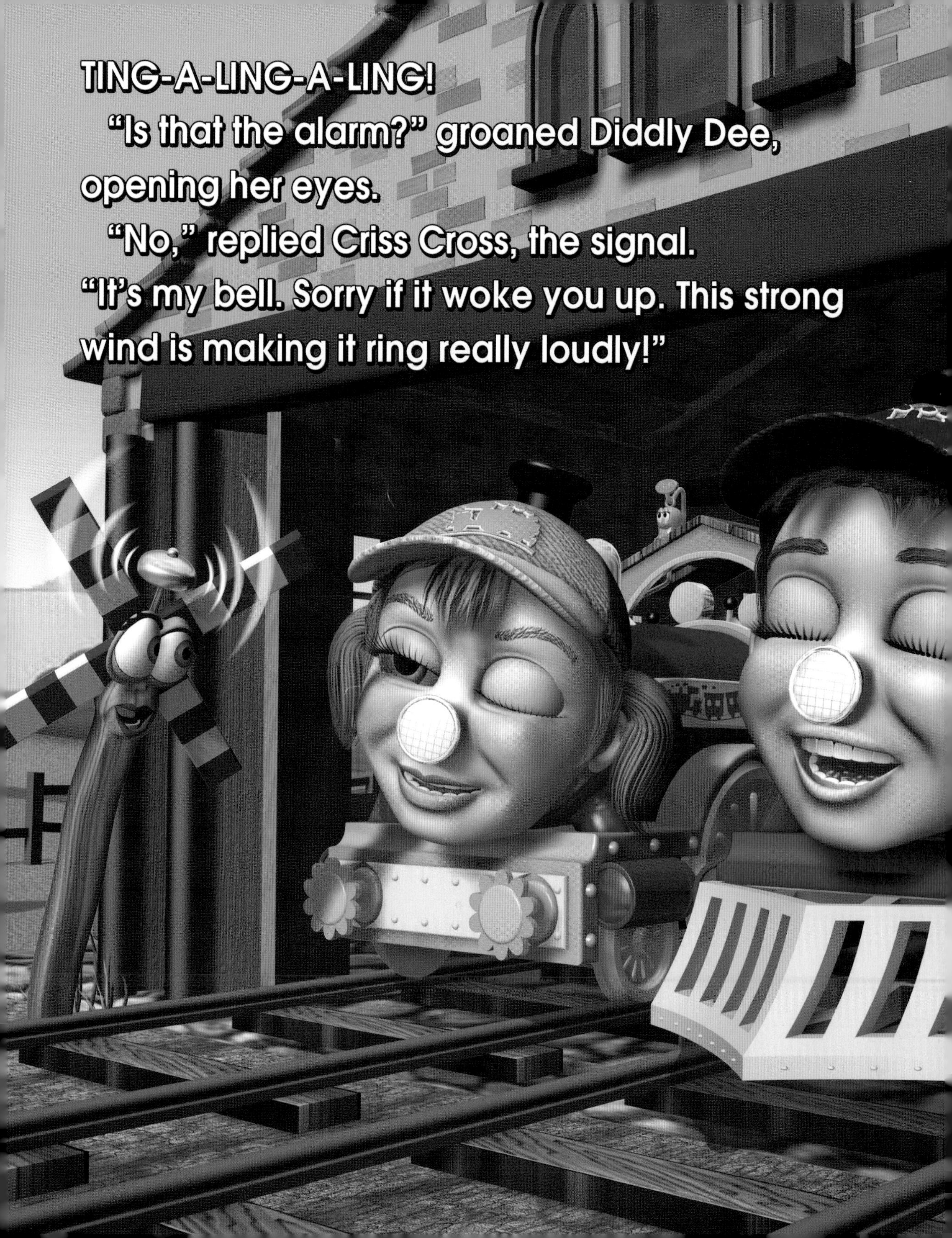

The wind was still blowing in powerful gusts when the train twins set off for Tootsville Station. On the way, they met Connor and Clair.

"Do you like our kites?" called Connor.

"We made them at school!" added Clair, proudly.

Diddly Dum wanted to watch the children flying their colourful kites, but his sister would not let him.

"Charlie is waiting for us," she scolded. "Come on!"

"Pity!" sighed Diddly Dum, disappointedly.

At the station, Flora had arrived to collect Charlie's washing.

"This windy weather is perfect for drying clothes," she chuckled.

Suddenly, the clock began to flash and the hands spun round and round.

"Someone needs help!" thought Charlie.

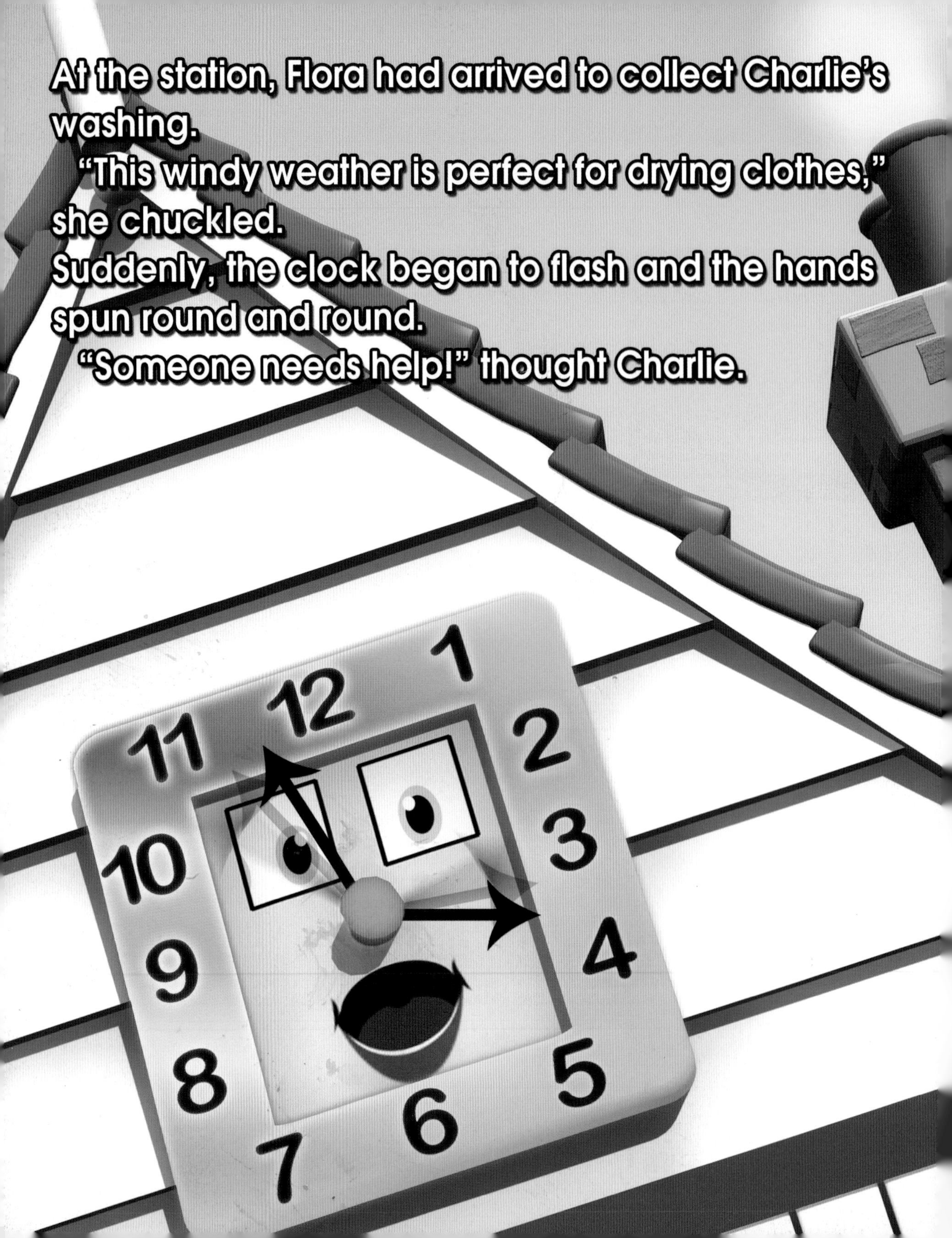

How could Charlie stop Flora finding out about the Diddlys' secret missions?

"Here's my jacket to wash!" he cried, taking it off and draping it over her head!

"Who put the lights out?" she wailed.

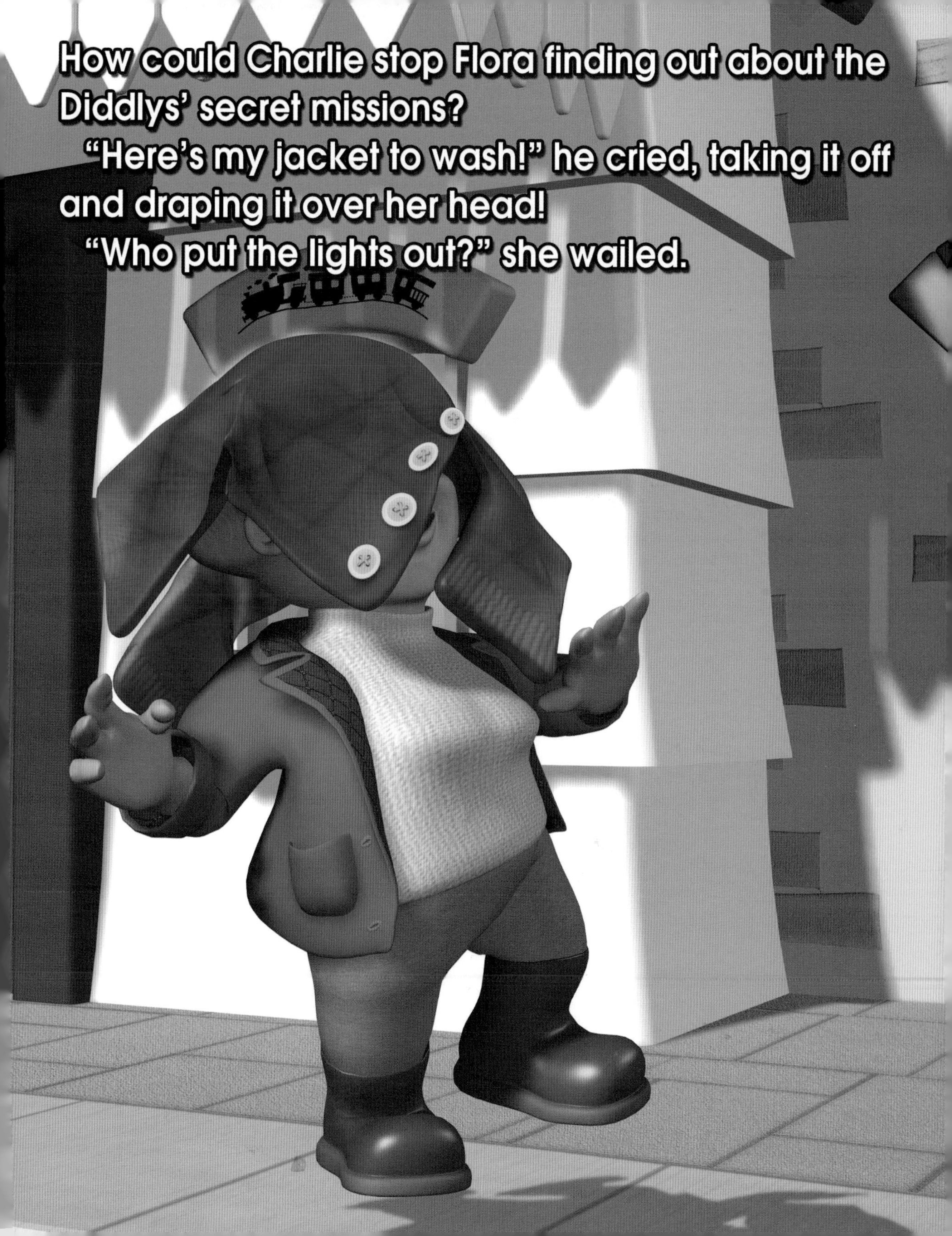

Quickly, Charlie pulled a lever and disappeared through the secret trapdoor. He slid down the chute and landed with a BUMP in his Control Room beneath the platform.

"*Must* find a better way of doing that!" he grumbled.

Hula, a lifeguard from the tropical island of Hawaii, was on the TV screen.

"A giant wave is coming!" he cried, urgently.

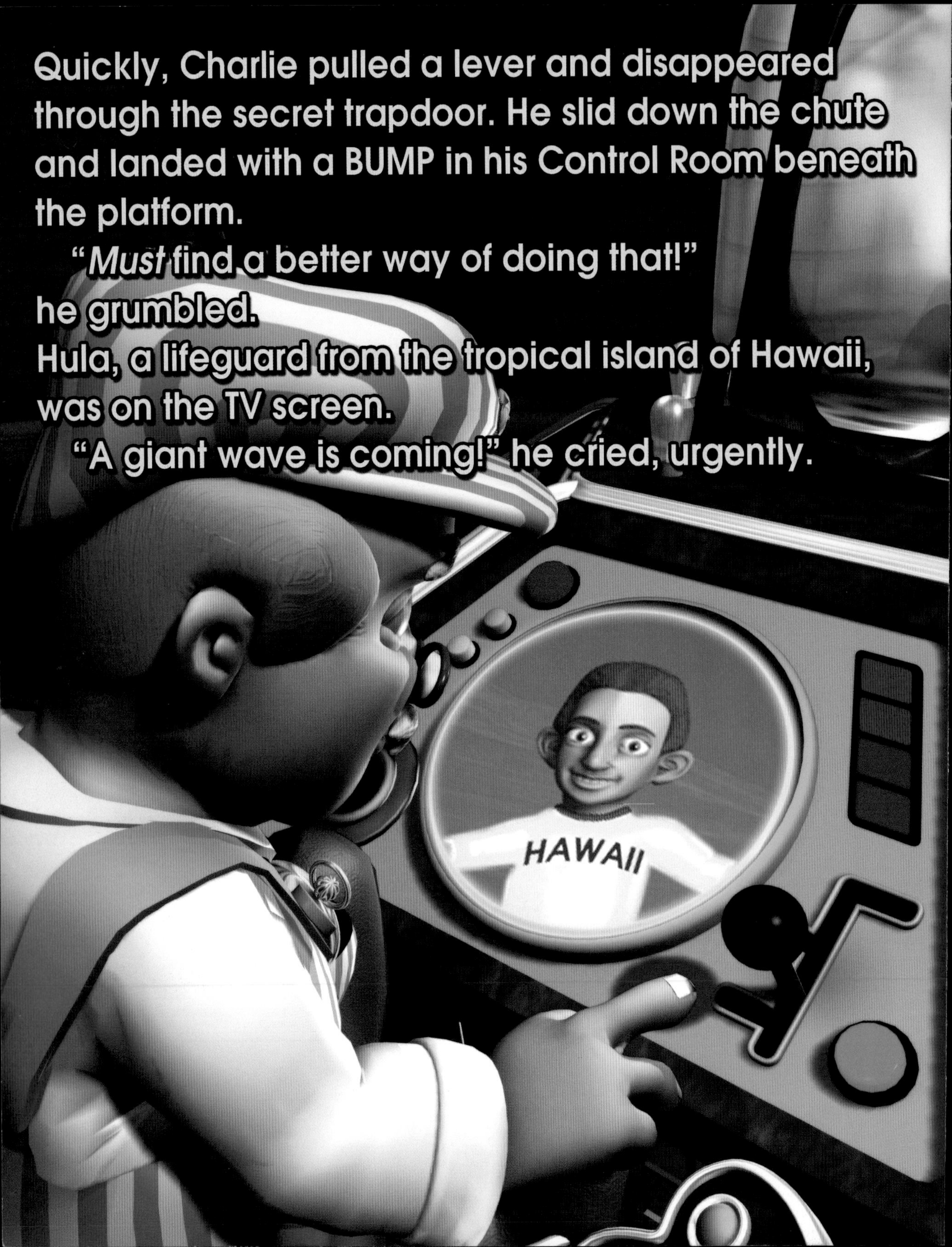

The wave had been whipped up by a powerful tropical wind and was heading for Waikiki Beach, putting surfers and holidaymakers in great danger. *Here was a job for the Diddlys!*

"I'm on my way, Charlie!" called Diddly Dum, speeding down the line towards the Magic Tunnel.

Inside the tunnel, H20 filled Diddly Dum with magic bubbles. THAKKA-THAKKA-THAKKA! The little steam train flew out the other end, changed into a *helicopter*!

"I'm flying over Hawaii now," he radioed back to Charlie.

"I can see the surfers and sunbathers on Waikiki Beach, but there's no sign of that big wave."

"Keep looking, Diddly Dum," advised the old station master.

Suddenly, Diddly Dum heard a loud roaring noise. Looking round, he saw the wave rolling towards him, white foam frothing along the edge.

"M-M-Mercy!" he gasped. "It's HUGE!"

How could Diddly Dum warn the holidaymakers to get out of the way in time?
WHIRR! CLICK! A loudspeaker came out of a panel in his side and positioned itself in front of his mouth.

"Just what I need!" he chuckled.

Diddly Dum zoomed down and hovered above the dazzling white sand.

"CLEAR THE BEACH!" he ordered, his voice booming and echoing all around. The holidaymakers saw the approaching wave and ran to safety on higher ground.

"Mission over, Charlie!" called Diddly Dum.

"Don't think so!" replied Charlie, who was watching everything on his TV screen. "What about the surfers in the sea?"

"I'd forgotten them!" gasped Diddly Dum.

Meanwhile, back at Tootsville Station, Mick the Milkman was showing Diddly Dee his model glider.

"Shall I launch it off the end of the platform?" he asked, excitedly. "It should fly well in this wind!"

Flora was pegging out her washing in the field next door.
WHEEE ... THUMP! The glider looped the loop and then collided with the bossy old lady.
"YEOWCH!" yelled Flora, leaping forwards.

Far away in Hawaii, Diddly Dum had a problem.

"I can't warn the surfers!" he yelled. "The roar of the waves is drowning my loudspeaker!"

"I'll send your sister to help you!" called Charlie.

Diddly Dee had to cut short her giggles as Flora chased Mick round and round the field!

"I'm on my way to the Tunnel now!" she radioed to Charlie, zooming along and puffing out smoke like a dragon.

Diddly Dee sped into the Magic Tunnel. H20 filled her with bubbles and WHOOSH! She shot out of the other end, changed into a high-powered *submarine*!

"Head for Hawaii as fast as you can," commanded Charlie.

A few moments later, Waikiki Beach came into view.

"I can see the surfers," called Diddly Dee. "They still haven't spotted the big wave behind them."

"Get them out of the way!" cried the worried station master.

VROOOM! Diddly Dee powered over to the surfers and told them the wave was coming. Then she sank down level with the sea.

"Hurry up, everyone!" she yelled. "Scramble onto my deck!"

Diddly Dee turned her motors to full power and tried to escape the huge breaking wave.

"There's n-n-nowhere to go!" she wailed.

"I can help!" called her brother, rescuing the surfers by lowering a rope ladder from above.

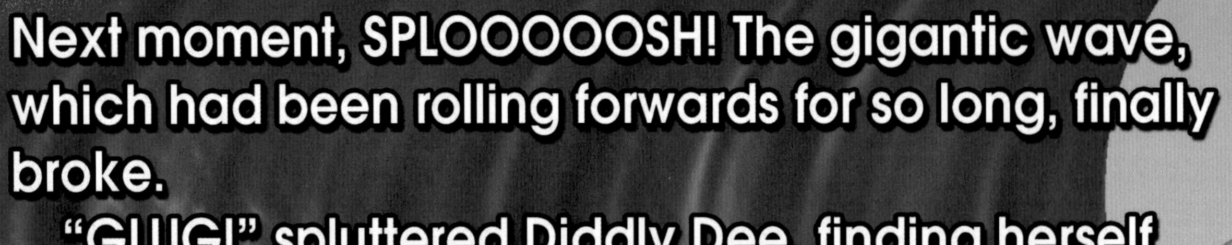

Next moment, SPLOOOOOOSH! The gigantic wave, which had been rolling forwards for so long, finally broke.

"GLUG!" spluttered Diddly Dee, finding herself going under a ten metre wall of white, foaming water.

"Come in, Diddly Dee!" called Charlie from his Control Room. "We've lost your picture. Where are you, Dee?"
There was no answer – just a blank TV screen making a high whistling noise!

From a high hilltop overlooking the beach, Diddly Dum with a rescued surfer, watched the massive wave crashing onto the sands below.

“We’re all safe, Charlie,” reported Diddly Dum. “But there’s still no sign of my sister!”

Everyone was very worried about Diddly Dee. Then, as the wave withdrew and the sea settled down again, a smiling face popped out of the water.

"Hi, guys!" chuckled Diddly Dee. "Did you miss me?"

Being a submarine, Diddly Dee had been perfectly all right beneath the waves!

"We've done our jobs now," she said. "So it's time to go home."

"Race you back to the Magic Tunnel!" laughed Diddly Dum.

H20 was waiting for the steam-powered superheroes and turned them back into railway engines again.

"Be careful," he warned. "It's as gusty as ever out there."

"Oh, bother!" exclaimed Diddly Dum. "The wind has caused us enough trouble for one day!"

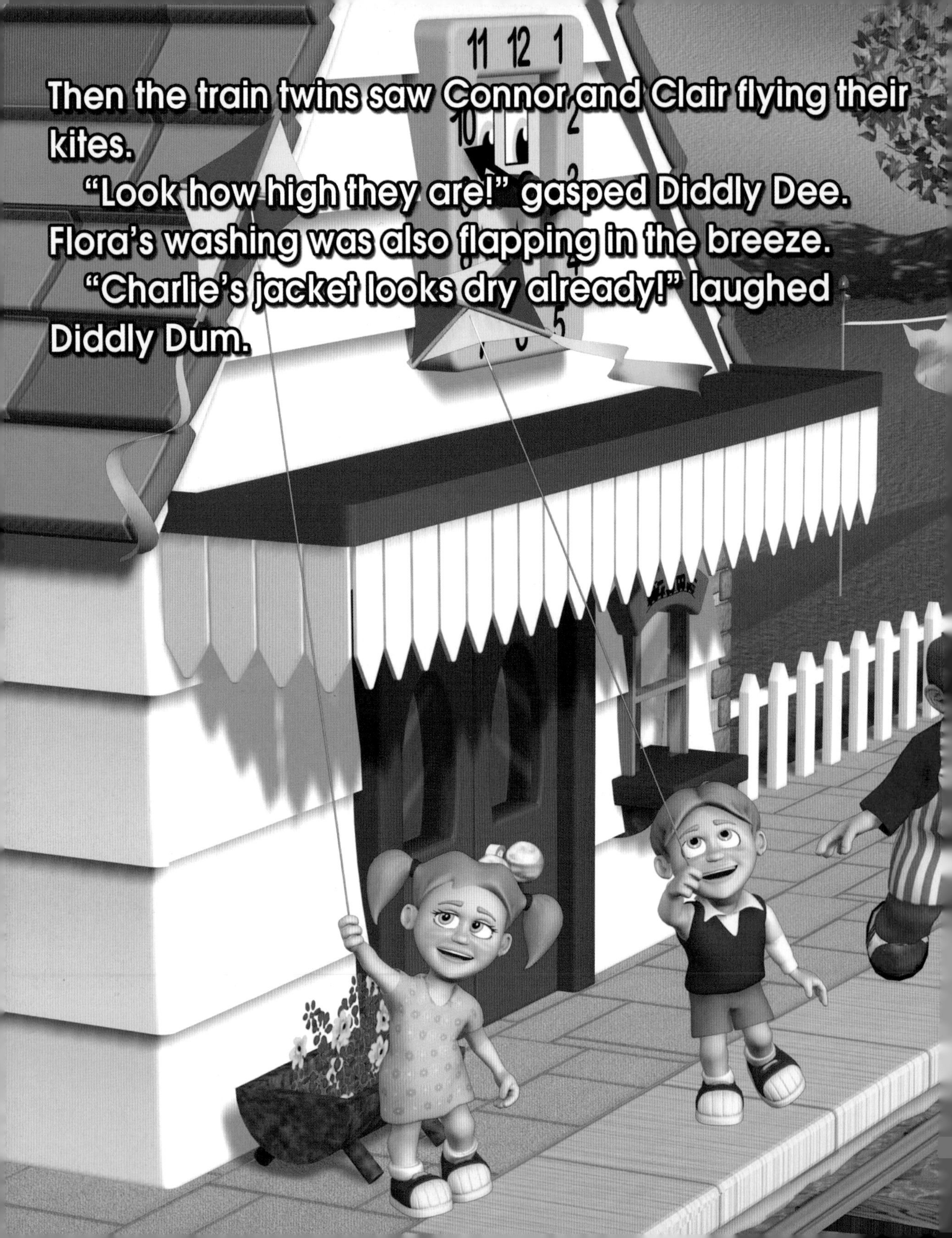


Then the train twins saw Connor and Clair flying their kites.

"Look how high they are!" gasped Diddly Dee. Flora's washing was also flapping in the breeze.

"Charlie's jacket looks dry already!" laughed Diddly Dum.

Finally, the trains stopped to watch Mick's glider soaring higher and higher in the sky. It looked just like a beautiful bird.

"Maybe the wind is not so bad after all!" agreed the little engines.

Later, Flora came round to return Charlie's jacket.

"Where are Diddly Dum and Diddly Dee?" she asked.

"I put some of your homemade ice-cream in their shed," laughed the old station master. "So they've gone home *like the wind!*"